FAIRY TALE COLLECTION

The
FISHERMAN
and HIS WIFE

RETOLD BY REBECCA FELIX
ILLUSTRATED BY KATHLEEN PETELINSEK

Published by The Child's World®
1980 Lookout Drive • Mankato, MN 56003-1705
800-599-READ • www.childsworld.com

Acknowledgments
The Child's World®: Mary Berendes, Publishing Director
Red Line Editorial: Editorial direction
The Design Lab: Design, production, and illustration

ISBN 978-1623236113
LCCN 2013931329

Printed in the United States of America
Mankato, MN
July, 2013
PA02179

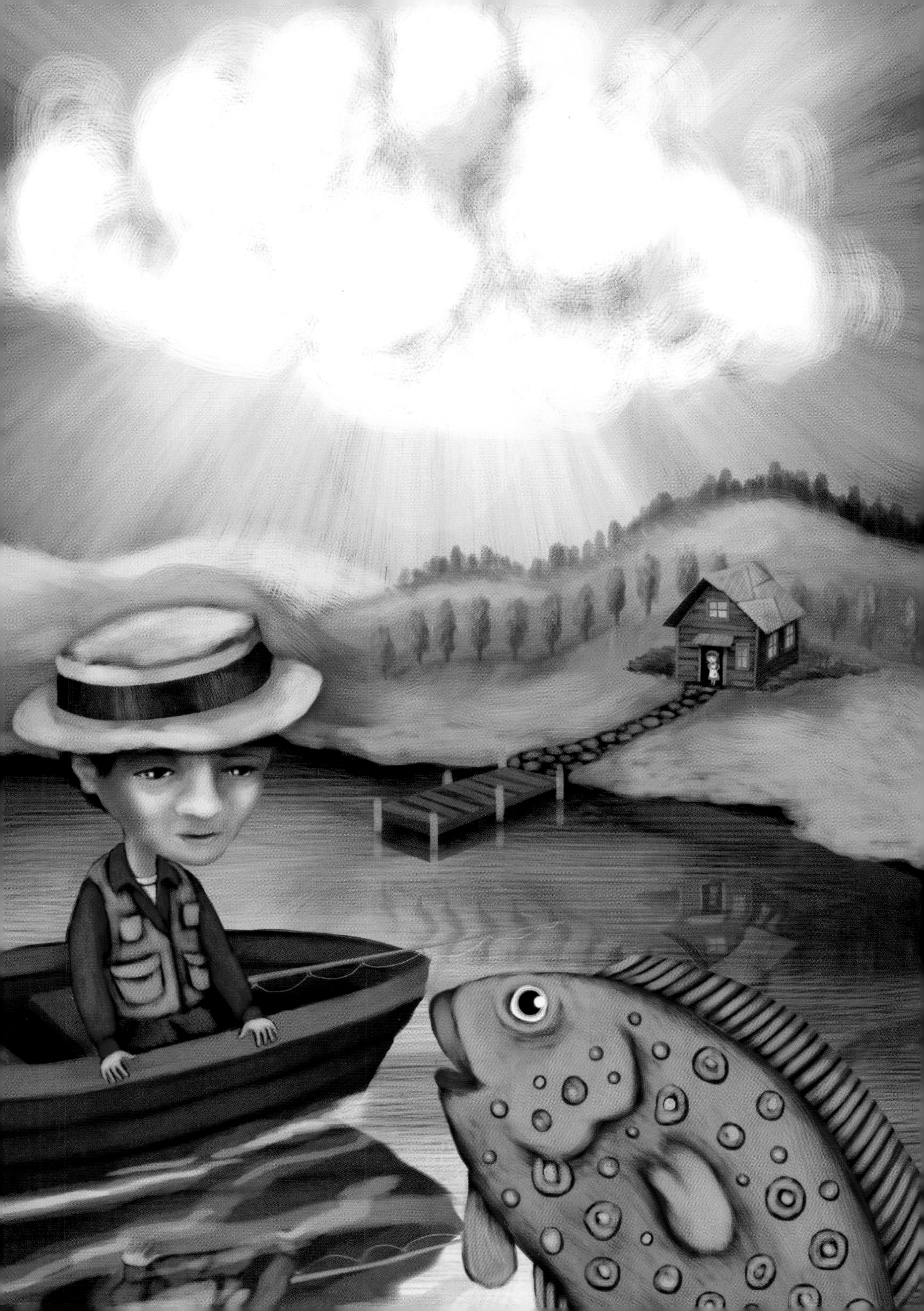

Long ago, near the sea, stood a tiny shack. A fisherman and his wife lived in this shack. Each day, the fisherman took his small boat out to sea. He fished all day, catching dinner for himself and his wife.

One of these days, the fisherman felt a strange tug on his line. His eyes lit up as the line stretched tight. The tug on the line was so strong that it tipped his boat toward the bottom of the sea, where his catch was trying to flee.

Using all his might, the fisherman pulled his catch to the surface. Up splashed a mighty fish, who looked the fisherman right in the eye.

"Please," spoke the fish, making the fisherman jump in shock.

"Please let me go, kind fisherman," continued the fish. "For I am no fish at all, but an enchanted prince under a spell."

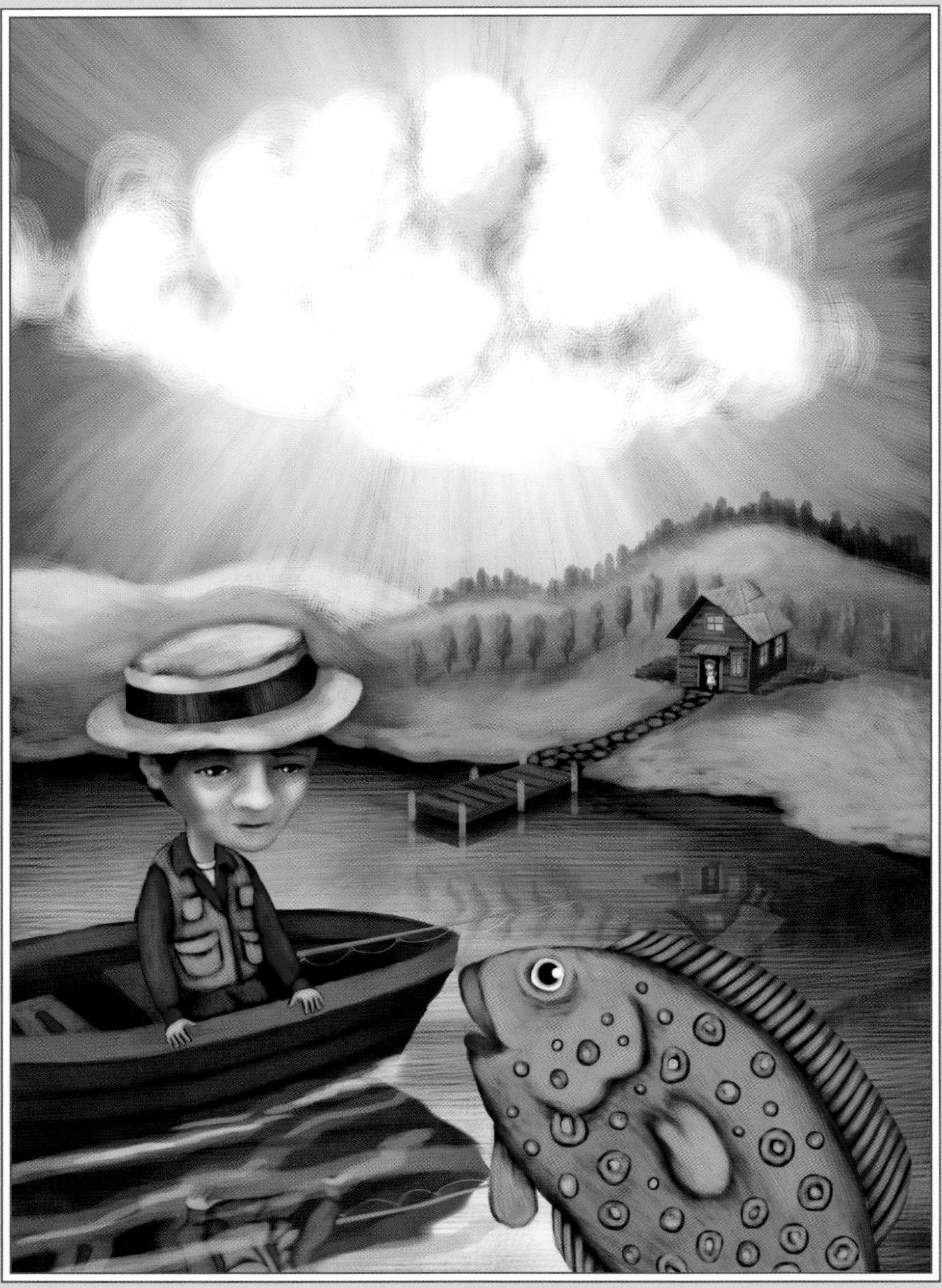

The fisherman had no plans to eat a prince. "Of course, kind prince," he said, and he released his hook and line. "Please, swim free."

The fish barely made a ripple as he dove back into the calm, clear water. Too shocked by these events to continue fishing, the fisherman turned his boat toward shore. He hurried back to his shack, excited to tell his wife about the fish.

But his wife was less than thrilled. "A what? And you *what*?" she yelled. "You caught an enchanted prince and let him go without asking for anything?"

"But what could he give? And for what would I ask?" the fisherman questioned.

"Enchanted princes grant wishes, you silly man!" shouted the wife. "And he owes us one for releasing him. Go back at once. Wish us out of this shack and into a cozy home."

The only thing the fisherman wished for was to avoid returning to the sea with such a demand. But his wife would not stop nagging him until he agreed.

Upon returning to the sea, the fisherman boarded his boat. He saw the water had turned a greenish yellow. He called over its surface,

Enchanted fish of the sea,

I once caught and released thee.

But now I'm made, by my wife,

to ask a wish improving life.

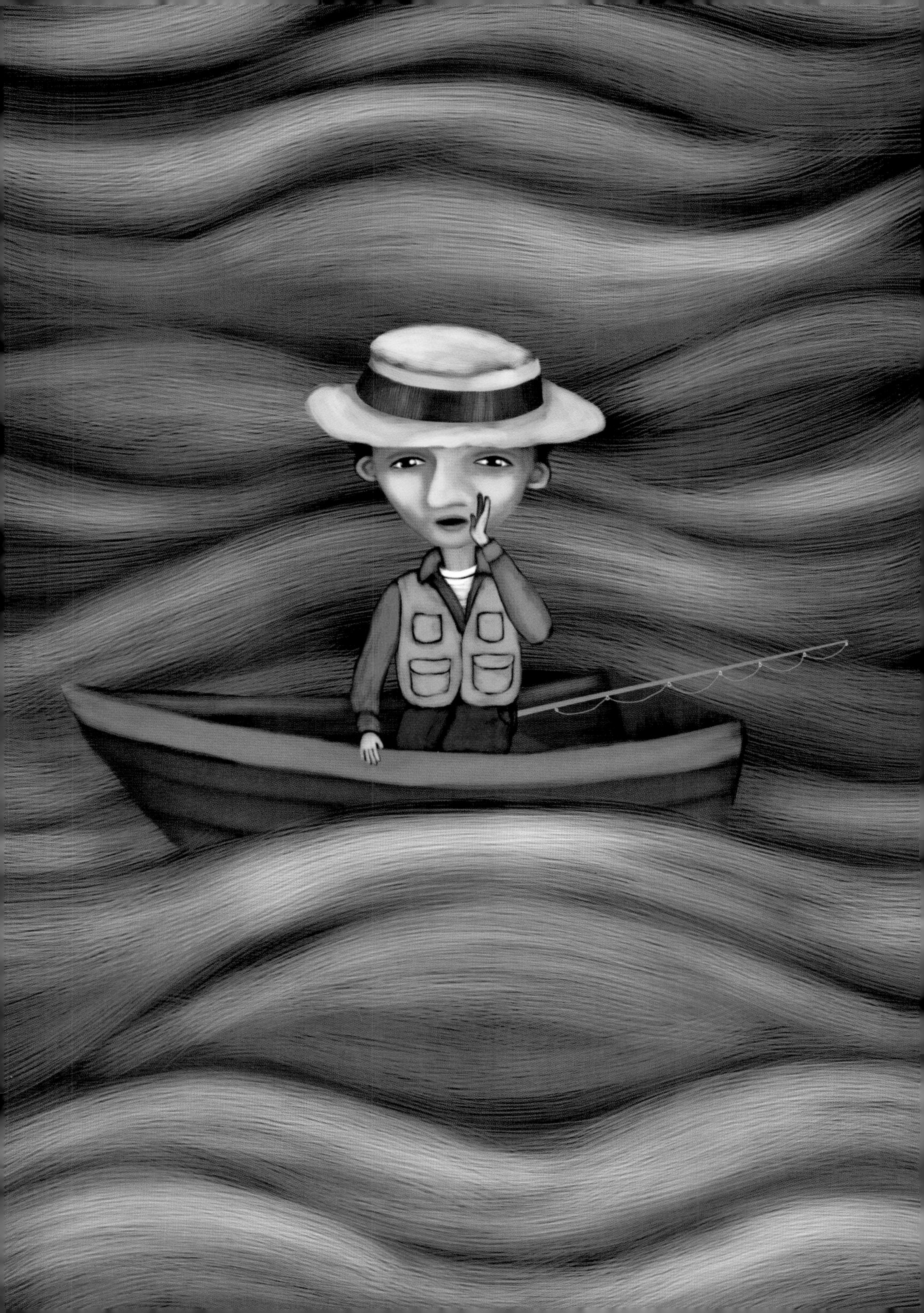

The fish appeared and asked, "What is it she wishes?" The fisherman quietly said she wished for a cozy home. "It is done," said the fish. "She is in the home now."

The fish dove beneath the sea before the fisherman could thank him. The fisherman returned to his home. But his home as he knew it was gone. A beautiful house with a stocked garden was tucked inside a tidy fence. His wife opened the gate and hurried him in. "Now this is a fine home," said the fisherman in wonder.

"I think it will do," said the wife. And it did—for a few weeks. But the wife grew tired of the home. She grew used to its walls and stocked garden. "Husband," she said one day. "This house just will not do. Go to the fish and ask that it might be made bigger and better."

The fisherman thought the house was wonderful as it was. And he felt it was not right to ask for more of the fish. But, as before, the woman would not stop asking until her husband agreed to go.

The fisherman approached the sea. He looked across the water. It had turned brown, as though mud swirled beneath the waves. The fisherman repeated his rhyming call over the water. Feeling ashamed, he delivered his wife's request when the fish came to the surface.

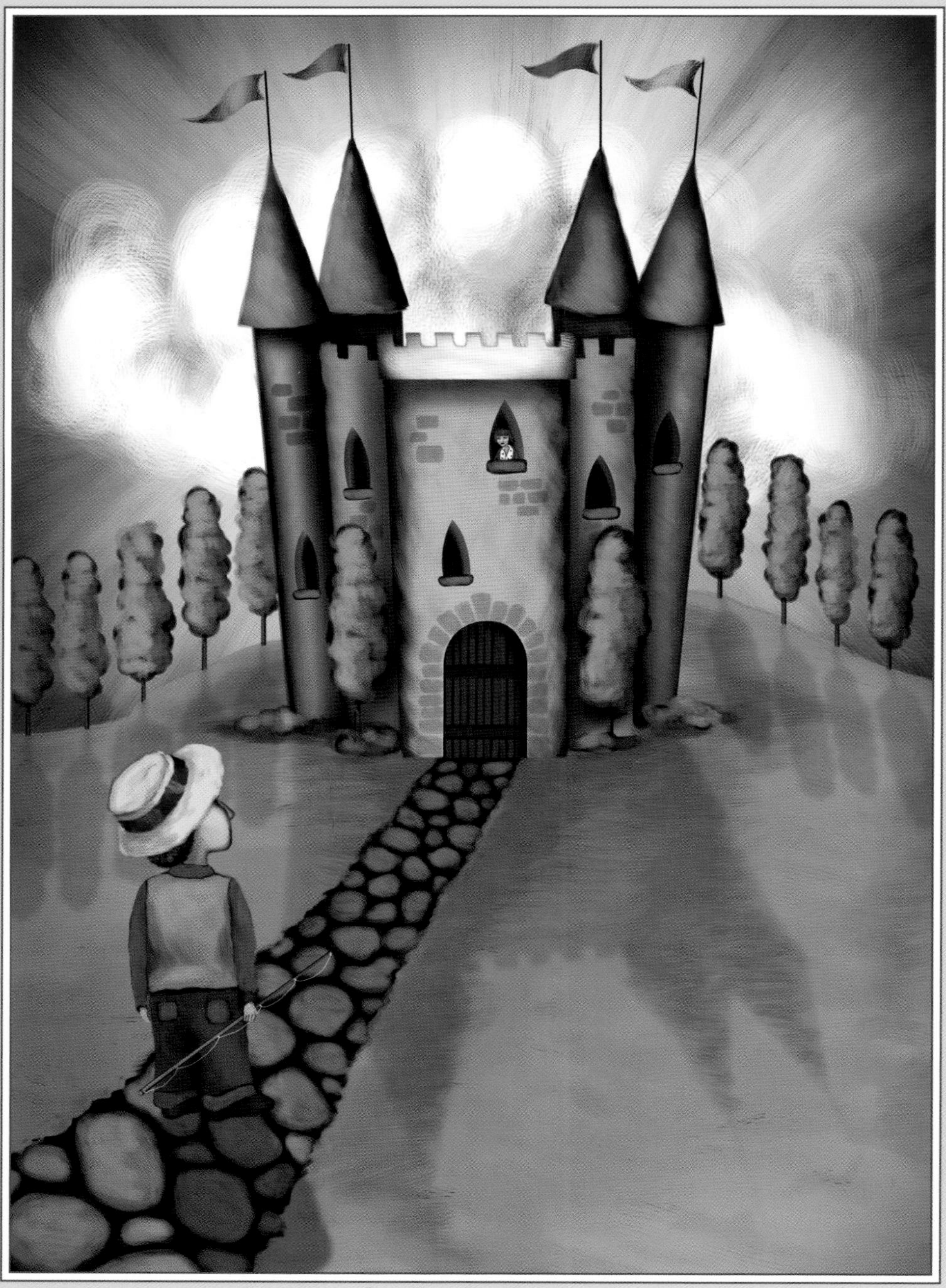

"Go to your home," said the fish. "You will find it is a castle. Your wife is there now."

The fisherman returned, and it was true. His home had grown into a mighty castle. It was three stories high and made of the finest stone. From the highest window, his wife called out to welcome him home.

"And a royal home it is!" said the fisherman. "It will do," replied his wife. Upon waking the next morning, the wife looked out from the highest window. She looked across the miles of rolling hills, the forests, and the farms.

Suddenly a castle was not enough. She wanted the land as well. She wanted not just to own it, but to *rule* over it!

"Oh, huuuus-baaaaand," her voice echoed through the castle. He rushed to her side. "Go see the fish and have him make us king and queen!" she demanded.

This made the fisherman sad. Was the castle not enough? It was not, she said. The fisherman did not want to be a king. But his wife did not care. She would be a queen. She argued with her husband until he agreed to return to the sea.

Onshore, the fisherman summoned the fish and repeated his wife's latest wish. "Okay, go home!" shouted the fish over churning waves. "She is a queen."

Being queen was fine enough—until that night. The fisherman's wife bothered him until he agreed to return and ask the fish for more. This time, the wife wished to be an empress.

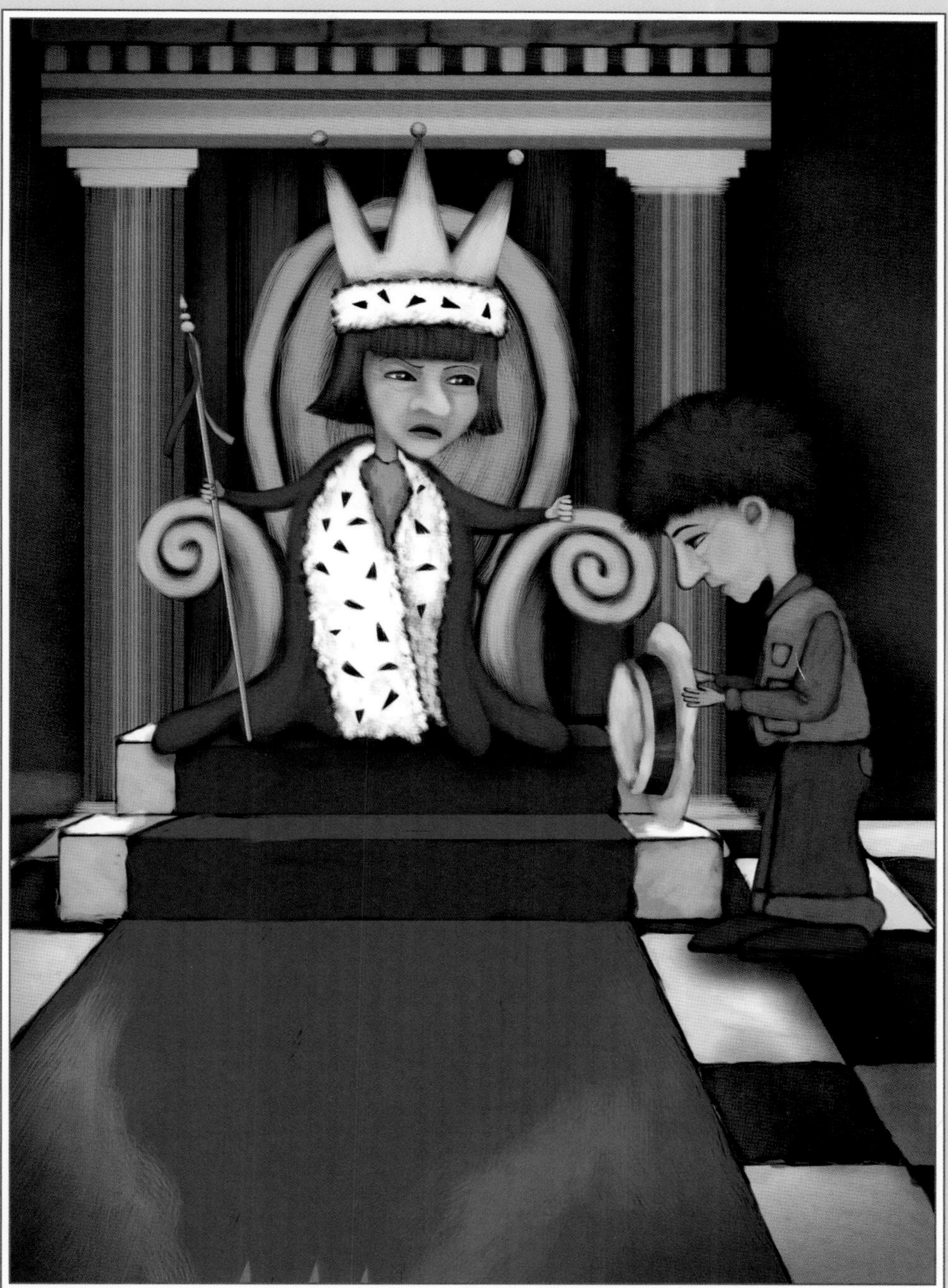

The fish granted this wish from frothy, foaming waves that were a dark and stormy gray. The husband returned home to find his wife in a gleaming gold chair. She was wrapped in silk with servants at her feet.

The fisherman had not been home more than one hour when his wife came to him. She now wished to be pope. The fisherman could not put up a fight. For as empress, his wife ruled him along with the empire's people.

The fisherman knew the fish was growing unhappy. He knew they should not ask for more.

He trudged to the sea. He shouted his lines to call the fish. His words were nearly lost in winds that whipped the waves into tornadoes a mile high. The fish surfaced between them

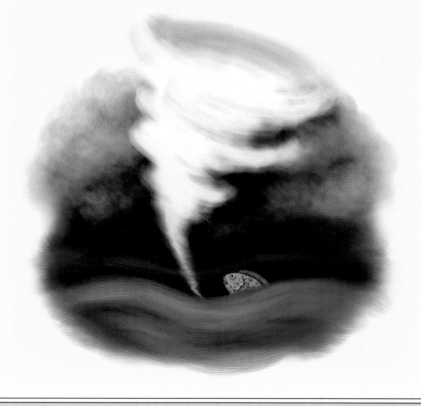

and granted the wife's wish. "She's pope!"
the fished screamed before disappearing into
the sea storm.

The fisherman ran from the angry sea.
But he was stopped at the door of the royal
home he shared with his wife, the pope.

"Turn back," she told her husband. "Pope is not good enough. I want to be as mighty as God."

The fisherman's eyes grew wide. He was more shocked by her newest wish than he was by the latest state of the sea. The water lunged toward him in waves as thick and black as oil.

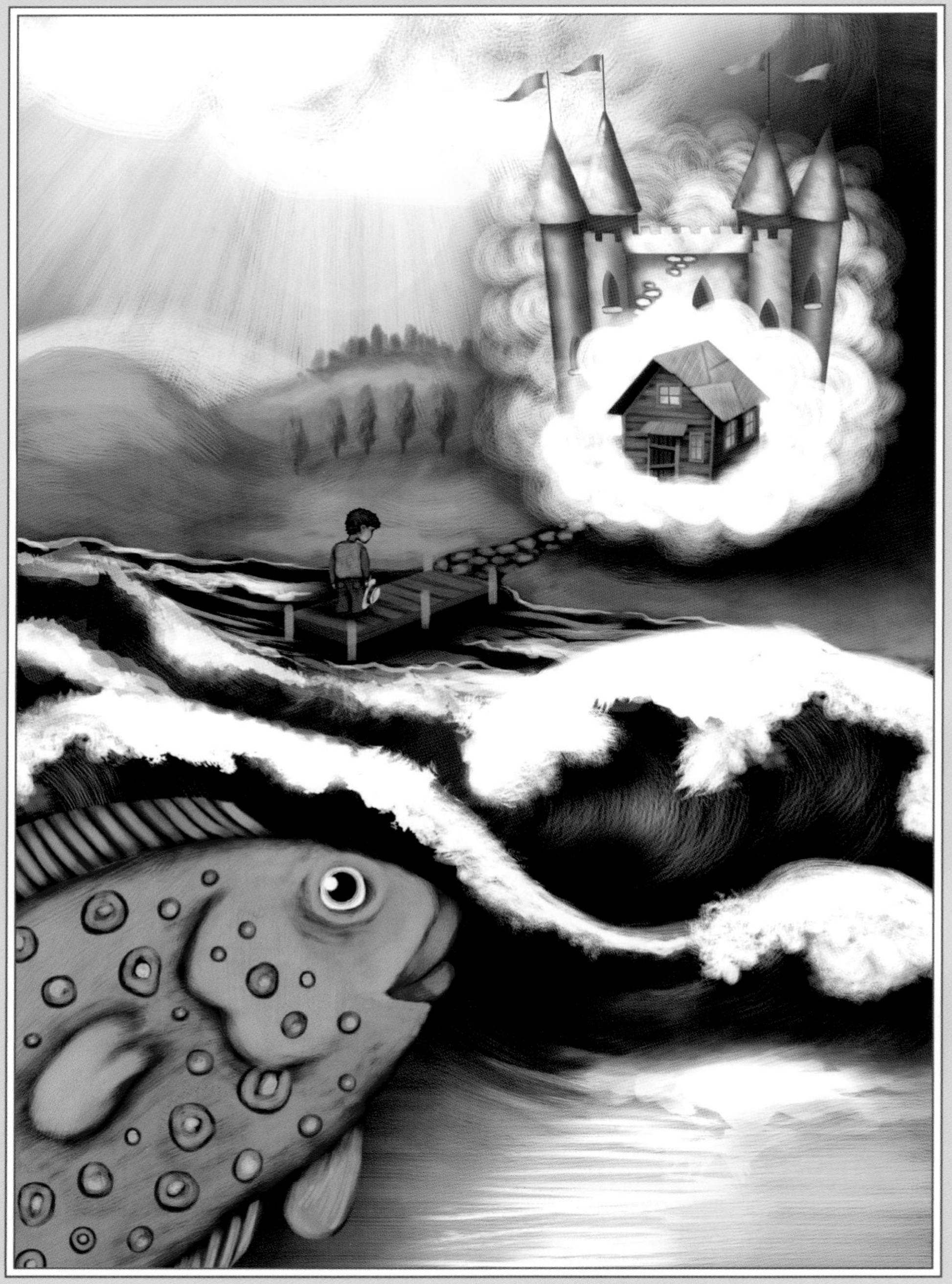

His familiar call came out as a whisper, so scared was he to ask the fish for this wish. But the fish heard him and rose from beneath the dark sea.

"Go home, fisherman," he said. "And see what has been done."

The fisherman was worried at what he would find. He hung his head the entire way. As he walked, the sea began to clear. When the fisherman reached home, he looked up and saw his wife standing outside their tiny shack. And there they lived the rest of their days, next to the calm and clear sea.

Fairy Tales

The story of the fisherman and his wife dates back many years. In 1812, Jacob and Wilhelm Grimm of Germany, better known as the Brothers Grimm, published a version of the tale. The Brothers Grimm traveled the world collecting stories, adding to them, and writing them down. Many of their stories have been told again and again, including "The Fisherman and His Wife." Although the words telling it are new, the main story is the same. What details would you add to this story if you were retelling it?

Just why do people retell this story? Certainly one reason is that it is entertaining. It is fun to hear about an enchanted prince who is a fish. And to picture the sea becoming darker and more violent as the wife asks for more and more.

But another reason many classic tales are retold is that they can teach us an important lesson. Why doesn't the fisherman want to ask the fish for his wife's wishes? Perhaps he thinks they are being ungrateful. Once the fisherman's wife has a taste of wealth and power, more is never enough. This tale cautions that people should be careful what they wish for. And that if we do not appreciate what we are given, it could all be taken away.

In the end, the fisherman and his wife are back in their tiny shack. We are left to wonder whether the wife realizes they had always had enough to be happy. What do you think? Do you think the wife was sorry? Do you think she found happiness with what they had?

About the Author

Rebecca Felix is a writer and editor. She lives in Florida, near the sea. She grew up reading classic fairy tales and loves working on children's books today.

About the Illustrator

Kathleen Petelinsek loves to draw and paint. She lives next to a lake in southern Minnesota with her husband, Dale; two daughters, Leah and Anna; two dogs, Gary and Rex; and her fluffy cat, Emma.